C0-AAW-052

Stories for 3 year-olds

BONNEY
PRESS

Contents

Published by Bonney Press
an imprint of Hinkler Books Pty Ltd
45–55 Fairchild Street
Heatherton Victoria 3202 Australia
www.hinkler.com

BONNEY
PRESS

© Hinkler Books Pty Ltd 2019

Authors: James Davies, Melissa Mattox, Clemency Pearce
Illustrators: James Davies, Michael Terry, Laura Hughes, Sarah Coleman, Lalalimola
Design: Aimee Forde
Prepress: Splitting Image

All rights reserved. No part of this publication may be reproduced, stored in a retrieval system, or transmitted in any way or by any means, electronic, mechanical, photocopying, recording or otherwise, without the prior written permission of Hinkler Books Pty Ltd.

ISBN: 978 1 4889 1446 1

Printed and bound in China

Welcome to
Stories for 3-year-olds

Storytime can be the snuggliest part of the day with your 3-year-old—and a good storybook can ignite your child's imagination and teach them lots about the world, and themselves!

Reading together is also one of the best things you can do for your little one's development. By age three, many kids are chatterboxes, holding simple conversations with a vocabulary that's growing in leaps and bounds— just like them! They may recognize some letters and words now—with a bit of help from you!—and are starting to learn their numbers. Reading aloud is one of the best ways to support them.

Stories for 3-year-olds contains three marvelous stories to enjoy with your child—especially chosen to be engaging for 3-year-olds, who can follow more complex tales. We've also included two fun nursery rhymes to finish with a flourish!

Lucy Loves Horses features a little girl many 3-year-olds will identify with. Lucy loves horses, and on her birthday her parents have a special surprise for her. But is it the horse she's begged for? This colorful tale about not quite getting what you want will have everyone giggling!

The Great Tortoise & Hare Counting Race is the perfect story to help your child with their numbers. Your child will love bouncy, impatient Hare and slow, kind Tortoise, who both love to count. Who will get to 20 first?

Finally, *The Beast Beneath the Bed* tackles a common bedtime fear and defuses it once and for all. Who could resist Laura Hughes's zany, brilliant illustrations of the fearsome beast as he wreaks havoc on Charles's bedroom? It's to become a storytime favorite!

Happy reading!

Lucy **loved** horses.

Not just a little...

...but a **lot!**

She had a
horse bike,

she had a horse bag,

she had

horse slippers,

but she
didn't have
a **horse**.

"Mooooooooooooom..." Lucy begged. "Please, please, please can I have a horse for my birthday?"

"Let's wait and see!" said Mom.

The morning of her birthday, Lucy raced downstairs to find a big pile of presents.
"None of these look like a horse," she thought.

"We have one last present for you," said Dad, "but you have to close your eyes!"

Lucy closed her eyes as tightly as she could...

"SURPRISE!"

"What is **THAT**!?" Lucy asked.
"It's a pony!" said Mom. "Don't you like him?
His name is Hamish."

"**THAT** is not a real horse," Lucy sulked.

Lucy didn't love Hamish,

but Hamish loved Lucy.

She tried to ignore him,

but he followed her everywhere.

The next day was Lucy's birthday party.

"We have one last surprise for you," said Mom.

It was a ride on a very **big**, very **tall** horse.

"I HATE HORSES! They're too big!" screamed Lucy.

26

Now, Lucy **loves** Hamish!

For my sister Rosie

To my son Eric – MM
To lovely Sam, welcome to the family – MT

The Great TORTOISE & HARE Counting Race

3
2
1

12
11
10

MELISSA MATTOX • MICHAEL TERRY

"I'm counting," says Tortoise.

"Counting? I **love** to count!"

"Me too! Now, please don't interrupt," says Tortoise. "**4, 5, 6** ..."

"**7, 8, 9**!" Hare shouts, bouncing up and down. "And... wait, what comes after **9**?"

"**10**," says Tortoise, "but don't count so fast."

But Hare doesn't listen.

"11, 12, 13, 14..." giggles Hare.

"Wait!" Tortoise shouts.

"**15, 16** ..." says Hare.

"Be patient," says Tortoise.
"I'm getting there."

"*Tortoise!*
What comes after **16**?"

"I must know!" sobs Hare.
"The suspense is **unbearable**!"

"This wait is exhausting!
I think I'll take a nap."

46

47

1 2 3 4 5

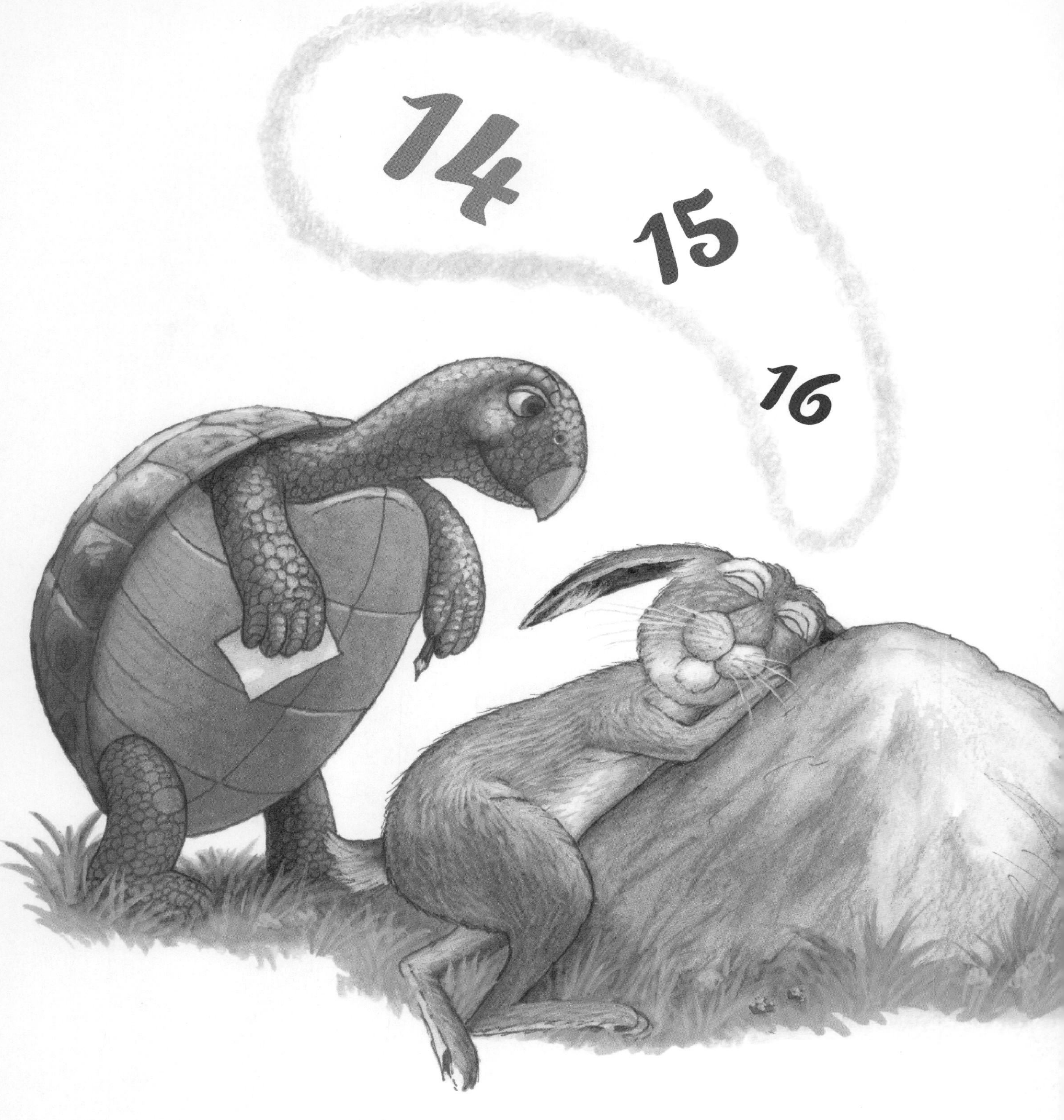
14
15
16

"Oh no, I overslept!" Hare wails. "Wait, what's this?"

"**17**! How could I forget you **17**? I love you **17, 18, 19**..."

"**20**", Tortoise says.

"I knew that," says Hare.

"Now, let's count backwards! **20, 19, 18, 17, 16...**"

"Hold on, I'm coming!" says Tortoise. "**15, 14, 13, 12...**"

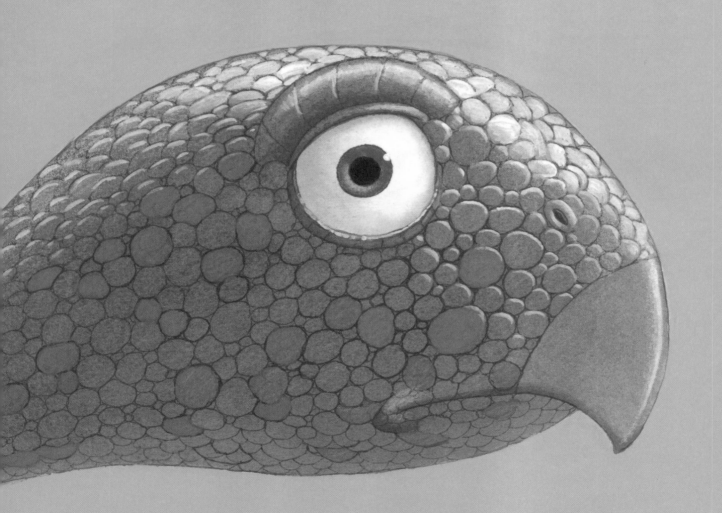

The
Beast Beneath
the Bed

Clemency Pearce

Laura Hughes

Each night when warmly snuggled down, when dreams are swirling in my head,

There comes a creepy, crawling noise...

SCRATCH

SCRITCH

...THE BEAST BENEATH THE BED!

The scratchy sounds and little growls echo in the dark.

I pull the covers to my chin and hear him cough and bark.

One day, I snuck a little peek, and saw the fearsome brute.

He was two-feet high, with bright red eyes. Anything but cute!

With tangled fur and awesome fangs, he really was a sight.

His claws were long and razor sharp; he gave me such a fright!

I watched, as he began to steal all my lovely toys.

He ate my smartest pair of shoes, then made a burping noise.

He tore right up the bookcase on lightning little paws.

He chomped on all my fairytales with ferocious snappy jaws.

He swung upon my lampshade,

"WHEEEEEEEEEEEEE!"

howling as he flew.

I'd never seen such naughtiness! My horror grew and grew.

Then he fell down,

"BUMP!"

and left a dent upon the floor.

He gobbled up my teddy bear...

...**THAT** was the final straw!

"STOP IT NOW, YOU FIEND!"

I yelled, leaping to my feet.

"You've messed up all my precious things and I like to keep them neat!"

At this the creature froze and stared. He was scared of me instead!

I found my fear had disappeared of The Beast Beneath The Bed.

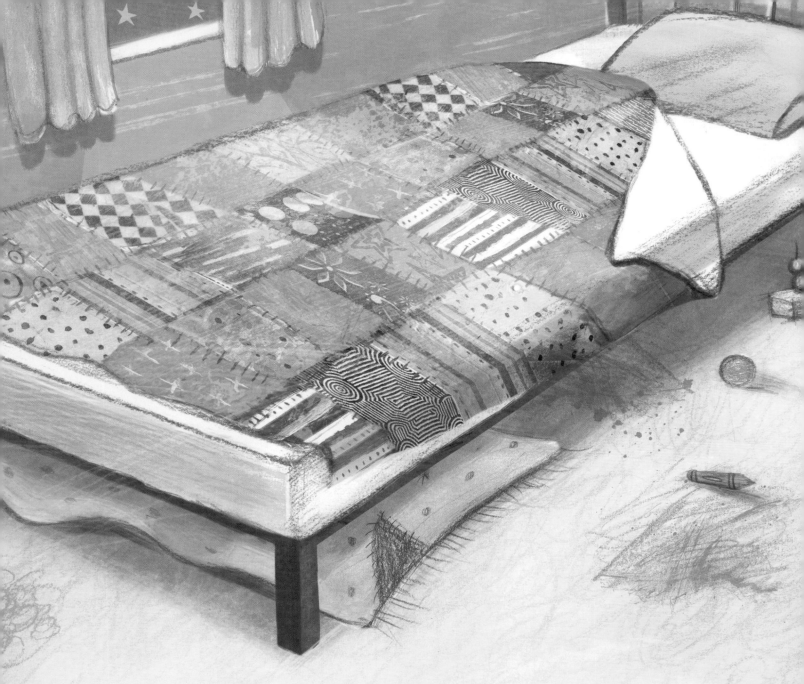

"Why are **YOU** so terrified? So petrified?" I said.

He replied, quite mystified,

"YOU'RE THE BEAST ABOVE MY HEAD!"

"When the sun shines bright and clear, and I'm snoozing
in my den,

You ruin all my magic mess by cleaning up again!"

We had both been naughty monsters, in very different ways.

He'd sabotaged my night-times...

and I'd haunted all his days.

So we put our heads together, and we made a special deal.

I'd let him play with all my toys, if he promised not to steal.

He said he wouldn't eat my shoes, if I left him out some bread.

And now there is no talk of beasts; we use proper names instead.

So when I'm drifting off at night, and hear those scratchy snarls,

I just say,

"MORNING, ROBERT!"

and he says,

"GOODNIGHT, CHARLES!"

The Grand Old Duke of York

Oh... the grand old Duke of York,
He had ten thousand men,
He marched them up to the top of the hill
And he marched them down again.
And when they were up they were up,
And when they were down they were down;
And when they were only halfway up,
They were neither up nor down.

Rub-a-dub-dub

Rub-a-dub dub,
Three men in a tub,
And who do you think they be?
The butcher, the baker,
The candlestick-maker.
Turn them out, knaves all three.